To JAS and JHF – lost, but not forgotten. — CRS

To Julia and Samantha, two fast friends. — RG

For Stan & Lily. — HL

Text copyright © 2020 by Corey Rosen Schwartz and Rebecca J. Gomez · Illustrations copyright © 2020 by Hilary Leung

ISBN 978-1-338-72957-3

10 9 8 7 6 5 4 3 2 1   20 21 22 23 24

Printed in the U.S.A.   40 · First edition, September 2020

Book design by Doan Buu

TWO TOUGH TRUCKS GET LOST!

by **COREY ROSEN SCHWARTZ** and **REBECCA J. GOMEZ**

illustrated by **HILARY LEUNG**

Scholastic Inc.

Two tough trucks,
the fastest of friends,
loved racing and chasing
and zipping 'round bends.

One day after school
they met up at the park.
Their folks said, "Stay close,
and be back before dark!"

RUGGED RIDE PARK

VROOM! ZOOM!

Through gravel and muck.
A daredevil dude and
a thrill-seeker truck.

They whooshed and
they whizzed
with rip-roaring speed.
"Which way are we going?"

"Just follow my lead!"

They zipped past an arch
and made a sharp turn.

"We're faster than lightning!"

"Burn, baby, burn!"

VROOM! ZOOM!

Mack dashed ahead.

A glimmer of blue and a flicker of red.

The trucks kicked up dust
as they passed an old mine,
and neither one noticed
the bright yellow sign.

"Woo-hoo!" hollered Mack
as he raced out of sight.

Then Mack headed left . . .
and Rig headed . . .
right.

SKID! SCREECH!

They stopped in their tracks.

A dumbfounded Rig and a mystified Mack.

One Mack, one Rig,
both looking around.

They searched and they searched
till they reached the same ridge,
but Rig took the tunnel
and Mack took the bridge.

VROOM! ZOOM!
Each truck on a ledge.
A Rig feeling rattled, a Mack on the edge.

Through canyons and quarries
they zigzagged and crossed.
"The sun's going down!"
"I'm hopelessly lost!"

One Mack on his own,
unwilling to yield.
"I'll search from this cliff.
I'll see the whole field!"

One Rig, all alone,
off-track in the park.
"I've got to find Mack.
He's afraid of the dark!"

GLOOM! DOOM!
Too tired to roam.
Missing each other,
longing for home.

One Rig, one plan,
one flickering flare.
"I hope Mack will see this."

"There's Rig over there!"

So Mack hurried back
to his best buddy's side.
"I'm so glad I found you!"
"Me too!" Rig replied.

ETCH! SKETCH!

They scratched on the ground,
drawing the places they'd driven around.

They backtracked through canyons,
they zipped past the cliff.

"Our folks must be worried."
"I bet they're scared stiff!"

They rounded a bend,
then Rig shouted, "Hey!
That arch looks familiar.

This must be the way!"

Two tough trucks
approached a bright light.

RUGGED RIDE PARK

Then Rig headed left,
and Mack headed right . . .
beside him.